ARROW BOOK OF
Spooky Stories

Edited by NORA KRAMER

Illustrated by Erwin Hoffmann

SCHOLASTIC BOOK SERVICES

Published by Scholastic Book Services, a division
of Scholastic Magazines, Inc., New York, N.Y.

For reprint permission grateful acknowledgment is made to:

Harper & Row, Publishers, Inc. for "The Ghostly Fisherman" from THE TALKING CAT by Natalie Savage Carlson, copyright 1942 by Natalie Savage Carlson.

David McKay Co., Inc. for "The Tinker and the Ghost" from THREE GOLDEN ORANGES AND OTHER SPANISH FOLK TALES by Ralph Steele Boggs and Mary Gould Davis, copyright 1936 by Longmans, Green and Co., Inc., now David McKay Co., Inc.

William Morrow & Co., Inc. for "The Dancing Jug" from THE WITCHES' RIDE AND OTHER TALES FROM COSTA RICA by Lupe de Osma, copyright 1957 by Lupe de Osma.

G. P. Putnam's Sons for "The Strange Visitor" from ENGLISH FAIRY TALES by Joseph Jacobs.

Story Parade, Inc. for "Horace the Happy Ghost" by Elizabeth Ireland, copyright 1951 by Story Parade, Inc.

Vanguard Press, Inc. for "The Stubbornest Man in Maine" from NEW ENGLAND BEANPOT: AMERICAN FOLK STORIES TO READ AND TO TELL by M. Jagendorf, copyright 1948 by M. Jagendorf.

Henry Z. Walck, Inc. for "A Shiver of Ghosts" from CHINESE MYTHS AND FANTASIES by Cyril Birch, copyright © 1961 by Cyril Birch.

The World Publishing Co. for "The Lucky Man" and "Here We Go" from THE THING AT THE FOOT OF THE BED AND OTHER SCARY TALES by Maria Leach, copyright © 1959 by Maria Leach; for "Never Mind Them Watermelons" from THE RAINBOW BOOK OF AMERICAN FOLK TALES by Maria Leach, copyright 1958 by Maria Leach.

Elizabeth Yates for "The Friendly Ghost" from SPOOKS AND SPIRITS AND SHADOWY SHAPES, copyright 1949 by American Book Co.

Single copy price 35¢ includes postage. Quantity prices available on request.

Copyright © 1962 by Scholastic Magazines, Inc.
1st printing . . . . September 1962
Printed in the U.S.A.

CONTENTS

ARROW BOOK OF
Spooky Stories

Horace the Happy Ghost

BY ELIZABETH IRELAND

Horace was a happy ghost. He lived with his father and mother in a big old house with lots of creaking stairs and windows that rattled. It was just right for ghosts.

Of course, people lived there too — a whole family of people — but they all got along very well together. The ghosts didn't mind the noise the people made daytimes, and the people didn't mind the noise the ghosts made at night.

There was only one trouble.

Horace!

Horace was a well-behaved little ghost in some

1

ways. He had learned his vanishing lessons perfectly. One moment he was there, and then — whisk! — he wasn't. Sometimes he vanished for his family's visitors at after-midnight tea, and they all said they had never seen finer vanishing. Besides, he could creak doors, and he rattled windows as a grown-up ghost.

But he couldn't moan, and he couldn't groan, and when he tried to clank his chain, it jingled!

"What is wrong, Horace?" his father and mother asked him often. "It's perfectly silly for a bright little ghost like you not to moan and groan. What is that horrible noise you make?"

"People call it laughing," Horace said. "I'm sorry. I just can't moan and groan. I'm too happy! I haven't anything to moan and groan about!"

His father and mother would groan softly, and float upstairs to talk things over.

Horace wandered around, creaking a stair or two and rattling at the second biggest window just for practice.

Once he laughed. When he did, the people upstairs woke up suddenly and sat up in their beds and said, "What was that?"

"Oh, dear!" Horace said to himself. And he put one hand over his mouth and kept it there till daylight to make sure he wouldn't laugh again.

"Horace," his mother said when he went upstairs to go to bed that morning, "today you must stay up at least till noon. Maybe that will teach you to moan and groan."

"All right, Mother," Horace said cheerfully. He felt a little queer inside, though. He had never been up after sunrise in his whole life.

He floated downstairs very slowly and started to haunt the breakfast room. He felt jiggly as he peeped inside for the first time. How bright it was!

And it was positively full of people laughing and talking and drinking milk and orange juice and eating breakfast food.

Horace took a deep breath, stepped out beside the kitchen cabinet, and vanished.

The littlest boy at the breakfast table saw him. He gurgled and waved his spoon. Horace vanished again beside the refrigerator.

"Funny thing," the father said, and rubbed his eyes. "I could swear the refrigerator door was open just a minute ago. But it isn't."

3

Horace vanished again behind a window curtain.

"Mother, there's a ghost behind the curtain," the next-to-littlest boy said.

"Finish your cereal, Tommy, and stop trying to fool me," the mother laughed.

And after that nobody paid any attention to Horace! Even when he laughed, somebody else laughed too, and nobody noticed him. Finally he perched on top of the refrigerator and watched the family finish breakfast.

Then he went outside. It was queer and scary in the bright sunlight with no nice comfortable dark, no big hoot owls and whippoorwills singing songs that Horace loved, and no dogs howling far over the hills. But pretty soon he found out he was getting used to the daytime and the songs of the other birds and all the queer daytime sounds. There wasn't a single thing scary about them, once you knew what made them.

He wandered around having a fine time, though he did get a bit sleepy. As the big grandfather clock struck noon, he whisked upstairs and woke up his mother.

She look at him anxiously. "Did you learn to moan and groan, Horace?"

4

Horace shook his head. "No. I found out that daylight is just as nice and friendly as dark!"

"Oh, dear!" his mother groaned. "Well, go to bed, Horace. But whatever you do, don't laugh! Mother needs her sleep. I've tossed and turned all day."

Horace went to his own room, yawning. He didn't laugh but he couldn't keep from chuckling a little bit.

That night his mother and father had a ghost visitor to after-midnight tea.

When she heard Horace laugh, she shrieked, "Dear me! What a horrible child! Really, he takes the curl right out of my hair. Why don't you do something about that laughing?"

"What can we do?" Horace's mother moaned.

"Shut him in a lighted room with lots of people," the visiting ghost snapped. "If that does not teach him to moan and groan, I don't know what will!"

"It sounds cruel," Horace's father said, "but I think we had better try it."

A week later, sure enough, Horace's mother marched him downstairs and opened the big living room door a tiny crack.

"There! Inside with you! And mind you stay at least an hour!"

5

Horace didn't come back up for three whole hours.
His mother was walking up and down, wringing
her hands, when he appeared.

6

"Oh, darling, I shouldn't have done it! Forgive me, Horace! Was it so terrible?"

"I had a wonderful time, Mother!" Horace said. "It was a Halloween party. Everybody was dressed up. There were three other ghosts like me, only I think they were really people. We played games. I won a prize, too. A horn!"

"Ooooh!" his father groaned. "Where is it? Did you learn to play it?"

Horace shook his head. "No. I gave it to another little ghost who couldn't vanish the way I did when we played hide-and-seek."

Horace's father and mother looked at each other and sighed.

"All right, Horace, go rattle your chain for a while," his mother said, "and *do* try not to jingle."

"Yes, Mother," Horace said happily and floated off.

"At least he didn't bring the horn home," his father said. "That's one thing to be thankful for."

Loud jingling sounded from the next room. Horace's father and mother groaned, clapped their hands over their ears, and vanished.

But the very next evening something happened.

7

Horace and his family woke up just at sundown and smelled something perfectly delicious!

"What is that *wonderful* smell?" Horace asked.

His mother and father exchanged a mysterious smile.

"It's ghosts' favorite food — and that's all I will tell you now," his father said.

And his mother said, "Hurry and put on a clean sheet. It looks as if we're going to have a party tonight!"

They floated downstairs in a great hurry, and out the hall to the kitchen. They stopped by the door.

In the kitchen Tommy was saying to his mother, "But what happens to the middle of the doughnuts, Mother?"

His mother laughed. "Why, doughnut middles are the favorite food of ghosts, Tommy! See that big bowl that looks empty? It's full to the top with doughnut middles!"

Horace jiggled up and down excitedly. He had often heard about doughnut middles, but he'd never eaten one. He could hardly wait to try them!

As soon as the people had taken their doughnuts to the dining room, the ghosts swished into the kitchen and began eating doughnut middles.

8

Horace's mother ate only two dozen, because she was on a diet. Horace's father ate four dozen.

And Horace finished the whole bowlful! Ummm, were they good!

But a little while later, when his mother and father looked for Horace, they couldn't find him anywhere. He wasn't in the cellar or the attic or the garden or downstairs.

At last they found him curled up in bed in his own room.

"Ooooh," he said, "I have a pain!"

"Horace!" his parents beamed. "You *groaned!*"

"OOOOoooooOOOO!" said Horace. "It *hurts!*"

"Horace!" His parents both hugged him. "You moaned, too!"

"Yes," Horace said, "because I have a pain in my middle. How about some spirits of peppermint or something? OOO! OOOOoooOOO!"

And ever since, Horace has been able to moan and groan beautifully. Even if he's happy, all he has to do is think about the time he ate too many doughnut middles. It always works.

But he still can't clank his chain!

9

Never Mind Them Watermelons

BY MARIA LEACH

Once there was a man who said he didn't believe
in ghosts, didn't believe in haunts, didn't believe in
haunted houses.

Another man said he'd give him a whole wagon-load of watermelons if he would spend the night in a certain old empty house down the road.

The man said, sure, he'd sleep there, so he picked up his matches and tobacco and set out. He went in the house and lighted his pipe. He sat down in a chair and started to read his paper.

Pretty soon something sat down beside him and said, "Ain't nobody here but you and me?"

"Ain't gonna be nobody but you in a minute," said the man. So he jumped out the window and started to run. He ran pretty fast, overtook two rabbits going the same way. Pretty soon something caught up with him and said, "Well, you makin' pretty good speed."

"Oh, I can run faster than this," said the man — and did.

When he passed the man who gave him the dare, he said, "Never mind about them watermelons."

The Tinker and the Ghost

A Spanish Ghost Story

BY RALPH S. BOGGS AND MARY GOULD DAVIS

On the wide plain not far from the city of Toledo there once stood a great gray Castle. For many years before this story begins no one had dwelt there, because the Castle was haunted. There was no living soul within its walls, and yet on almost every night in the year a thin, sad voice moaned and wept and wailed through the huge, empty rooms. And on All Hallow's Eve a ghostly light appeared in the chimney, a light that flared and died and flared again against the dark sky.

Learned doctors and brave adventurers had tried to banish the ghost. And the next morning they had been found in the great hall of the Castle, sitting lifeless before the empty fireplace.

Now one day in late October there came to the little village that nestled around the Castle walls a brave and jolly tinker whose name was Esteban. And while he sat in the market place mending the pots and pans, the good wives told him about the haunted Castle. It was All Hallow's Eve, they said, and if he would wait until nightfall he could see the strange, ghostly light flare up from the chimney. He might, if he dared go near enough, hear the thin, sad voice echo through the silent rooms.

"If I dare!" Esteban repeated scornfully. "You must know, good wives, that I — Esteban — fear nothing, neither ghost nor human. I will gladly sleep in the Castle tonight, and keep this dismal spirit company."

The good wives looked at him in amazement. Did Esteban know that if he succeeded in banishing the ghost the owner of the Castle would give him a thousand gold *reales?*

Esteban chuckled. If that was how matters stood, he would go to the Castle at nightfall and do his best to get rid of the thing that haunted it. But he

13

was a man who liked plenty to eat and drink and a
fire to keep him company. They must bring to him a
load of faggots, a side of bacon, a flask of wine, a
dozen fresh eggs and a frying pan. This the good
wives gladly did. And as the dusk fell, Esteban
loaded these things on the donkey's back and set out
for the Castle. And you may be very sure that not
one of the village people went very far along the
way with him!

It was a dark night with a chill wind blowing and
a hint of rain in the air. Esteban unsaddled his donkey and set him to graze on the short grass of the
deserted courtyard. Then he carried his food and his
faggots into the great hall. It was dark as pitch there.
Bats beat their soft wings in his face, and the air felt
cold and musty. He lost no time in piling some of

14

his faggots in one corner of the huge stone fireplace and in lighting them. As the red and golden flames leaped up the chimney Esteban rubbed his hands. Then he settled himself comfortably on the hearth.

"*That* is the thing to keep off both cold and fear," he said.

Carefully slicing some bacon he laid it in the pan and set it over the flames. How good it smelled! And how cheerful the sound of its crisp sizzling!

He had just lifted his flask to take a deep drink of the good wine when down the chimney there came a voice — a thin, sad voice — and "*Oh me!*" it wailed, "*Oh me! Oh me!*"

Esteban swallowed the wine and set the flask carefully down beside him.

"Not a very cheerful greeting, my friend," he said, as he moved the bacon on the pan so that it should be equally brown in all its parts. "But bearable to a man who is used to the braying of his donkey."

And, "*Oh me!*" sobbed the voice. "*Oh me! Oh me!*"

Esteban lifted the bacon carefully from the hot fat and laid it on a bit of brown paper to drain. Then he broke an egg into the frying pan. As he gently

15

shook the pan so that the edges of his egg should
be crisp and brown and the yolk soft, the voice came
again. Only this time it was shrill and frightened.

"Look out below," it called. *"I'm falling!"*

"All right," answered Esteban. "Only don't fall into
the frying pan."

With that there was a thump, and there on the
hearth lay a man's leg! It was a good enough leg and
it was clothed in half of a pair of brown corduroy
trousers.

Esteban ate his egg, a piece of bacon and drank
again from the flask of wine. The wind howled
around the Castle and the rain beat against the
windows.

Then, *"Look out below,"* called the voice sharply.
"I'm falling!"

There was a thump, and on the hearth there lay a
second leg, just like the first!

Esteban moved it away from the fire and piled on
more faggots. Then he warmed the fat in the frying
pan and broke into it a second egg.

And, *"Look out below!"* roared the voice. And
now it was no longer thin, but strong and lusty.
"Look out below! I'm falling!"

"Fall away," Esteban answered cheerfully. "Only don't spill my egg."

There was a thump, heavier than the first two, and on the hearth there lay a trunk. It was clothed in a blue shirt and a brown corduroy coat.

Esteban was eating his third egg and the last of the cooked bacon when the voice called again, and down fell first one arm and then the other.

"Now," thought Esteban, as he put the frying pan on the fire and began to cook more bacon. "Now there is only the head. I confess that I am rather curious to see the head."

And: "LOOK OUT BELOW!" thundered the voice. "I'M FALLING — FALLING!"

And down the chimney there came tumbling a head!

It was a good enough head, with thick black hair, a long black beard and dark eyes that looked a little strained and anxious. Esteban's bacon was only half cooked. Nevertheless, he removed the pan from the fire and laid it on the hearth. And it is a good thing that he did, because before his eyes the parts of the body joined together, and a living man — or his ghost — stood before him! And *that* was a sight that

17

might have startled Esteban into burning his fingers with the bacon fat.

"Good evening," said Esteban. "Will you have an egg and a bit of bacon?"

"No, I want no food," the ghost answered. "But I will tell you this, right here and now. You are the only man, out of all those who have come to the Castle, to stay here until I could get my body together again. The others died of sheer fright before I was half finished."

"That is because they did not have sense enough to bring food and fire with them," Esteban replied coolly. And he turned back to his frying pan.

"Wait a minute!" pleaded the ghost. "If you will help me a bit more, you will save my soul and get me into the Kingdom of Heaven. Out in the courtyard, under a cypress tree, there are buried three bags — one of copper coins, one of silver coins, and one of gold coins. I stole them from some thieves and brought them here to the Castle to hide. But no sooner did I have them buried than the thieves overtook me, murdered me and cut my body into pieces. But they did not find the coins. Now you come with me and dig them up. Give the cop-

18

per coins to the Church, the silver coins to the poor, and keep the gold coins for yourself. Then I will have paid for my sins and can go to the Kingdom of Heaven."

This suited Esteban. So he went out into the courtyard with the ghost. And you should have heard how the donkey brayed when he saw them!

When they reached the cypress tree in a corner of the courtyard: "Dig," said the ghost.

"Dig yourself," answered Esteban.

So the ghost dug, and after a time the three bags of money appeared.

"Now will you promise to do just what I asked you to do?" asked the ghost.

"Yes, I promise," Esteban answered.

"Then," said the ghost, "Strip my garments from me."

This Esteban did, and instantly the ghost disappeared, leaving his clothes lying there on the short grass of the courtyard. It went straight up to Heaven and knocked on the Gate. St. Peter opened it, and when the spirit explained that he had paid for his sins, gave him a cordial welcome.

Esteban carried the coins into the great hall of the

Castle, fried and ate another egg and then went peacefully to sleep before the fire.

The next morning when the village people came to carry away Esteban's body, they found him making an omelette out of the last of the fresh eggs.

"Are you alive?" they gasped.

"I am," Esteban answered. "And the food and the faggots lasted through very nicely. Now I will go to the owner of the Castle and collect my thousand gold *reales*. The ghost has gone for good and all. You will find his clothes lying out in the courtyard."

And before their astonished eyes he loaded the bags of coins on the donkey's back and departed.

First he collected the thousand gold *reales* from the grateful lord of the Castle. Then he returned to Toledo, gave the copper coins to the *cura* of his church, and faithfully distributed the silver ones among the poor. And on the thousand *reales* and the golden coins he lived in idleness and great contentment for many years.

The Lucky Man

BY MARIA LEACH

Once there was a man lying in bed asleep. And
he woke up. He heard something flapping.
He got up. He walked softly to the window.
And he saw it.

22

It was white — flapping in the moonlight. It was under a tree. It would flap its arms out in the moonlight and then slip back into the shadow of the tree.

"It's a ghost," thought the man. "I'll fix him before he gets into the house."

Very stealthily he took his gun down off the wall where he hung it at night. And he shot holes in the flapping thing, one after another. But it went on flapping.

At last the man went back to bed. If he hadn't killed it, at least he had scared it, he thought, for it stayed in the shadow of the tree and came no nearer.

In the morning the man got up and went downstairs. His wife was already in the kitchen.

"You fool!" she said. "Shooting your clean nightshirt full of holes!" (She had washed it the day before and hung it in the tree to dry.)

"My nightshirt!" said the man. "Gosh! Lucky I wasn't in it!"

The Stubbornest Man
in Maine

A New England Ghost Story

BY MORITZ JAGENDORF

There lived a rich man near Booth Bay in Maine who was the stubbornest man in all the state.

His name was Bill Greenleaf, and when he made up his mind about something nobody could outargue him. He was as stubborn as a mule. He'd say his say, and no man could make him say different. Everybody agreed that his stubbornness would only end when he went to the better world, where maybe the angels would teach him a little giving in.

One day Bill Greenleaf called his family around him and told them his time had come. Said he:

"I've called you together to tell you I don't fancy being buried in thick, black earth. I want to be buried in shiny white sand straight from Davenport Bay. From Davenport Bay and no other place." That was a fine bay quite a distance from Squirrel Island where Bill's house stood.

"It's to be from Davenport Bay, and don't you forget it," he repeated over and over again.

His wife promised it would be done, and Bill Greenleaf died that very night.

At the first peep of dawn Widow Greenleaf sent a big scow with eight strong men to Davenport Bay to bring back enough fine, shiny white sand to bury her late husband, just as he had asked.

The day was clear, and the wind was right, but the scow was heavy, and it was a long, long way to Davenport Bay.

Spoke Peleg who was at the front oar:

"My arms are aching. We must row this long distance only to please a stubborn dead fellow who can't be stubborn no more. Sand's sand if it is from Davenport Bay in Maine or out in China Bay."

Michael, who was holding the oar alongside him, agreed.

25

"You're right, Peleg," he said. "Can't see why we have to suffer from Bill's stubbornness, now he's good and dead."

Moses, who was behind him, pulled hard on his oar, nodded his head, and added:

"We needn't pay any mind to his talk no more. He can't order us now telling us what he wants and what he don't."

"Reckon the widow won't know the difference between one kind of sand and another. Maybe she don't care neither," added Reuben.

"Let's get the sand right from that place there," cried Jabez, a tall red-haired fellow, pointing to a little inlet right in front of them.

The others agreed at once.

They swung the heavy scow toward land, and soon the flat bottom of the vessel scraped the white sand of the shore.

The men took the shovels with a good will, worked hard, and in quick time the vessel was full of the white sand. Then they turned homeward.

Now, when they had set out in the early morning, the sun was shining and the wind was gentle. But no sooner did they begin rowing back than there was a quick turn in the weather. The sun rushed behind black clouds, the winds came wildly from the four sides of the compass, and the bay turned into a churning sea.

Reuben and Peleg, Moses and Jabez, and all the others couldn't figure out how it came about, for there had been no sign or warning of a storm.

Rowing was hard. The big, heavy, flat-bottomed scow just wouldn't go at all. It lurched and bobbed like a sailor on a spree. At first the sand in the scow flew about in the faces and eyes of the men. Then waves began pouring in over the sides. The rain came down and made the sand brown and soggy and heavy as lead.

The storm raged worse and worse. The rain was whipping. The wind was screeching like painted Indians on the warpath. The men in the scow were wet and weary and madder than hornets.

Suddenly they saw through the rain a big figure flapping ghostlike.

It was swaying with the squalls, coming nearer and nearer to the boat. The rowing men turned as white as the foam that topped the waves. They stopped dead, and just held onto the sides while the scow lurched and dipped and seesawed like crazy.

The big thing was wearing a greatcoat. Nearer and nearer it came, with arms and coat flapping wildly in the tempest. Now it was near enough for

28

all to see a stubborn white face sticking out from the big white collar.

And whose face do you think it was!

Jabez roared louder than the racing wind:

"It's old Bill Greenleaf come back!"

He could say no more. His mouth and throat were so dry that all the water in the bay and all the rain from the sky couldn't take away the dryness. The other men felt no better. They were too scared to say a word.

But Bill Greenleaf had plenty to say:

"Aye, you guessed right! Trying to cheat me just because you think I'm dead and gone. I'm dead, all right, but I ain't gone yet."

He flapped his arms and bellowed like thunder:

"Take warning! Dump that mud-sand and row down and get a scowful of Davenport Bay sand just as I stipulated. In Davenport Bay sand I'm going to be buried and no other, mind. And don't take no year of Sundays but do it quick or I'll send you down so deep in the bay you'll drown for all your life."

There was a fast streak of lightning in the sky right then, and just as fast were Jabez, Peleg, Moses,

Reuben, and the others dumping shovelfuls of sand into the bay. It wasn't sweet work, for the sand was heavy as rocks, but the men never noticed it.

Old Bill Greenleaf, swaying in the wind, looked on and never said another word.

Funny thing, the less sand there was in the scow, the quieter the wind was over the water and . . . the thinner Bill Greenleaf became.

When the scow was empty and no speck of sand left in it, Bill Greenleaf was gone — and so was the storm.

The men in the scow never said a word. Maybe it was because they were tired, or maybe they thought doing was better than talking. They rowed with all their might to Davenport Bay and loaded the sand fast as a barn a-burning. They rowed back just as fast, loaded the sand in carts, and brought it back to bury Bill Greenleaf.

That's why people still say Bill Greenleaf is the stubbornest man in all of Maine. For in no other state did anyone ever hear of a man who was as stubborn when he was dead as when he was alive.

Here We Go!

BY MARIA LEACH

Once there was a rich farmer who had a fine farm, fine horses and cattle, a fine big house, and a fine wife and several children. He was a very happy man — happy, that is, except for one thing. There was a boggart in the house.

Boggart is a north-of-England word for a kind of trick-playing spirit which takes up its abode in people's houses and barns. Some say it is a ghost, and some say it is just a mischief-maker. It never really hurts anyone, but it can play a lot of painful practical jokes.

This farmer and his wife had a boggart. It used to walk around in the house at night and pull the

31

covers off people. It used to knock on the door
and when the sleepy farmer got up and went downstairs to open it, there would be nobody there.

It used to fall downstairs in the dark, making an awful racket, and when the wife ran into the hall, fearing it was one of the children, all the children would be safely in bed.

Sometimes it would just tap, tap, tap in the night on the lid of the linen chest. Sometimes it would roll a heavy ball across the floor, time and again, so no one could sleep, or let it go bump-bumping down the stairs. One night it threw all the pots and pans down the cellar stairs. That was a clatter!

Once in a while the boggart would pitch in and help the family. It would wash the dishes when the farmer's wife wasn't looking; or sometimes it would churn the butter or collect the eggs. It would feed and water the cows and horses. But more often than not it would tie knots in their tails or let them loose in the night so the farmer had to go looking for them. Once it broke all the cups and saucers.

One of its favorite tricks was to blow all the smoke back *down* the chimney whenever anyone tried to light a fire. Or it would blow out the match just when someone was trying to make a light.

At last the farmer and his wife got tired of all this. They could put up with a prank now and then.

But this boggart was so annoying and troublesome that something had to be done.

So they decided to move. They decided to move to a new house on a big farm far away where there would be no boggarts.

The man and his wife and children packed up all their belongings and piled them high on the big wagon.

Just as they were about to drive off, a neighbor came by and said, "Oh, are you moving?"

"Yes," said the man. He explained that the boggart's tricks had at last become unbearable. They could not stand their boggart any longer, so they were moving.

So the neighbor wished them luck, and they drove off. Then from the top of the load they heard a little voice say happily, "Well, here we go! We're off!"

34

The Friendly Ghost

BY ELIZABETH YATES

Julie had never been away from home before
and her first night in the country was a frightening
one. Of course, she knew Aunt Anna and Uncle
Harry well for they had often come to the city to
visit her parents. But this was the first time she
had been at the farm and Julie wasn't at all sure
that she was going to like making friends with
horses and cows and chickens. She wished she
hadn't come. She wished she could go home to-
morrow. She wished — Julie put her hands up to
her eyes. She didn't want to cry. She was nine years
old now and that was much too old to cry, but she

did feel lonely and strange as she stood in the middle of her room before she got ready for bed.

There was a knock at the door. "May I come in, Julie? I've got something for you." It was Uncle Harry's cheerful voice.

"Ye-es," Julie said, swallowing quickly and trying to smile.

"I've brought you some apples in case you get hungry in the night." Uncle Harry set the plate with three polished red apples on it on the little table by the window. "They're the first of the crop. I just picked them today. Aren't they beauties?"

"Ye-es," Julie said.

"Aren't you going to undress soon?"

"Ye-es," Julie said.

Uncle Harry looked out the window of the small ground floor bedroom. "I used to have this room when I was a boy," he said. "I always liked it because I could watch the horses and cows in the pasture. How would you like to ride one of the horses sometime, Julie?"

Julie clapped her hands together. "I'd like that."

Uncle Harry nodded. "Ned is the steadiest one, but Daisy is all right if she likes you."

"How would I know if she likes me?"

"Oh, you'll know all right, 'cause she'll come right up to you of her own accord."

After Uncle Harry left the room, Julie began to think that life in the country might not be so lonely after all. She undressed quickly and had just got into bed when Aunt Anna came in to say goodnight.

It was a mild August night but it would be cooler by morning, Aunt Anna said as she tucked the little girl in and leaned over to kiss her.

"Sleep well, darling, and don't be alarmed if you hear noises in the night. An old house creaks now and then."

"Why?" Julie asked, holding tight to Aunt Anna's hand as she did not want her to go.

"It's just the way the boards have of talking to themselves, telling about the things they've seen."

"Does it mean there are ghosts?"

"Mercy no, child," Aunt Anna laughed. "Whoever put such an idea in your head?"

But long after Aunt Anna left the room, Julie wondered about that. She lay wide awake in the darkness and the air coming in the window near the head of her bed ruffled the white curtains. Outside

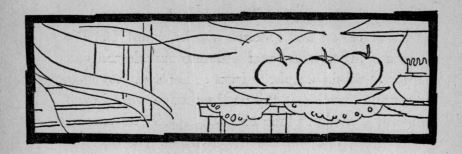

there were crickets chirping and katydids singing, but inside everything was quiet — or almost quiet.

Now and then a board in the floor gave out a small sound and another one in the wall would answer it. Julie shut her eyes tight, not wanting to see what might be in her room, but quite sure that something was. A cold little shiver began to run down her spine, for all the world as if someone had taken a dipper of water from the bucket by the well and poured it down her back. Julie opened her eyes for a moment, daring herself to look, but in the darkness she could see nothing. She wished that morning would come soon, and then she thought that she would eat one of the apples Uncle Harry had put on the table by her bed.

She sat up and reached out her hand, but just as she did so she heard a thump outside the window. And then, right in front of her eyes, she could see the curtains at the window move, very slowly, while something long and thin and white reached into the room, across the table by the window. Julie screamed and pulled the bedclothes over her. Then she dived down to the foot of the bed.

Aunt Anna and Uncle Harry heard the muffled screams of the little girl and came running down the stairs. They switched on the light in Julie's room and threw back the bedcovers.

"It was a ghost, I know it was," Julie said, her teeth chattering as she tried to tell them what had happened.

Aunt Anna comforted her and said there weren't any such things as ghosts except in people's imaginations.

Uncle Harry laughed easily. "Well, I guess I know one little girl who shouldn't eat apples before she goes to sleep."

"But I d-didn't eat an apple," Julie insisted. "I was just g-going to."

"That's funny," Uncle Harry said, "for I'm sure I put three apples on the plate and now there are only two."

Aunt Anna stared at the plate. "Perhaps you ate one yourself, Harry, for I certainly polished three apples."

Julie looked longest of anyone at the plate. "I know I didn't eat one," she said.

It was decided that Aunt Anna should sleep with Julie the rest of the night. She slipped into the big bed beside the little girl and cuddled her close. They whispered for a while together until they both began to feel sleepy.

Suddenly Julie pressed Aunt Anna's hand tightly. "What's that?"

"Just a board in the floor," Aunt Anna answered drowsily. "You'll get used to sounds like that in an old house."

Julie felt comforted, though she did not close her eyes again for a while. Instead she watched the curtains fluttering at the window. She was not afraid now because she knew that if that long white Thing reached in through the window she could waken Aunt Anna and the two of them could send it away.

But nothing happened and before long Julie fell asleep.

At breakfast, they all laughed about the strange visitor. Even Julie found it quite easy to joke about ghosts in daylight. Uncle Harry said it must have been a dream, and Aunt Anna said it was probably Julie's imagination. But neither of them could explain why, when there had been three apples on the plate, there were only two left.

Aunt Anna settled it for herself finally by saying, "You must have eaten one in your sleep, dear."

Julie shook her head. If she had, where were the core and the seeds?

That first day in the country was an active one for Julie. She helped Aunt Anna in the house and then she helped Uncle Harry outdoors, feeding the chickens and picking up apples in the orchard. She sat on the pasture bars and watched the two farm horses, wondering when Uncle Harry would let her ride one of them. She liked brown Ned, but it was the white mare Daisy who had Julie's heart. In the afternoon, Julie went berrying with Aunt Anna. By the time evening came she was so full of

41

sun and August wind and good times that she was quite ready for bed.

Aunt Anna said to Julie, "No ghosts tonight, dear. If you do see or hear anything, remember that it's just the wind at the window or the old boards in the house."

Julie was too tired to think about ghosts and far too happy. She lay in bed with her eyes almost closed, remembering all the wonderful things she had done that day. When a board creaked in the floor, she smiled to herself and thought how friendly it was to have a house so old that it could speak to one. She thought perhaps if she listened long enough that she would be able to tell what it was saying and then she would talk back. But she was much too sleepy tonight to do that.

And then, suddenly, she wasn't sleepy any more and her eyes that had been half shut were wide open. The curtain began to move at the window and the long white Thing that she had seen the night before came into the room.

Julie didn't waste any time screaming. She simply shot under the bedcovers and pulled them down around her at the foot of the bed. Whatever the

Thing was, she had seen it with her eyes and she was afraid that the next minute it would speak to her. She hardly dared move under the covers. But she decided not to take any chances and she did not put her head out until morning.

When Aunt Anna came in to wake Julie, she found her sleeping like a rabbit in its burrow, curled up at the foot of the bed with the sheets and the blankets all higgledy-piggledy.

Julie told her what had happened. "It was a ghost," she whispered. "I know it was."

Aunt Anna laughed right out loud. "You are a silly little girl. You ought to know that there aren't any such things as ghosts, not in this house anyway."

And then she looked at the plate on the table by the bed and smiled. "Why, Julie, you've eaten another apple! Uncle Harry will be glad that you like them so much."

Julie looked at the table for the first time that morning and her eyes grew as round as saucers.

The plate had only one apple left on it.

There were pancakes for breakfast and, somehow, laughing and talking with her aunt and uncle, the mystery of the night began to seem rather far away from Julie.

That afternoon, Uncle Harry took Julie by the hand and they went to the barway together. He called to the two horses and when they came up to him he slipped their bridles on and asked Julie which one she would rather ride.

"I'd like to ride Daisy," Julie said.

Uncle Harry shook his head. "Daisy doesn't make friends easily, but perhaps she'll be all right with you."

He lifted Julie up on to the mare's broad back. Then he got on brown Ned and together they ambled off to round up the cows for the milking. Uncle Harry nodded his head in surprise when he saw how gentle the horse was with the young girl from the city.

"I guess you've been making up to my old Daisy on the quiet," he said.

Julie shook her head and ran her hand down Daisy's neck. She was glad that Uncle Harry wouldn't have to think she was scared of everything, for the shuddering things that had been happening at night had made her a little ashamed of herself.

45

That night Julie went bravely to bed. Aunt Anna offered to sleep downstairs with her, but Julie said she would rather not. She felt quite certain now that she must have been dreaming for she knew there couldn't be any ghosts in a house as nice as the one her aunt and uncle lived in. Nobody believed her when she said she hadn't eaten the apples. So puzzled was Julie by their disappearance that she had begun to wonder if perhaps she had eaten them in her sleep — cores, seeds, and all.

"Good night, Julie dear, and I hope you won't have any dreams at all tonight," Aunt Anna said.

Julie was so tired and happy that she didn't spend any time at all lying awake and thinking. Instead she went sound asleep; nor would she have awakened before morning if sometime during the night she had not heard a curious sound. Feeling something warm near her face, she opened her eyes.

Moonlight was filling the room and in its soft glow Julie could see clearly that something had thrust its head in the window. She sat up in bed and a lump of fear rose right into the middle of her throat. She opened her mouth to scream, to call out for her aunt and uncle. Then suddenly she saw who it was: Daisy!

Julie put out her hand and stroked the long white head. Then she ran her fingers over the velvet nostrils that had bent so near her that she could feel the warm breath coming through them.

"Hello, Daisy," she said softly. "That was a nice ride we had, wasn't it? I hope we can have one like that every day."

Daisy tossed her head and gave a little neigh.

Julie wished she had a lump of sugar to give the horse, but she explained to Daisy that she would bring one to the barway the next morning.

"Do you like apples?" she asked, remembering that there was one left on the plate.

But when she looked at the plate she saw that it was empty!

Slowly a wide smile spread over Julie's face, "I guess you *do* like apples," she said.

Daisy drew her head back from the window and whinnied. Then she flicked her back feet and Julie saw her trotting across the grass, taking the low pasture bars in her stride.

Uncle Harry and Aunt Anna could scarcely believe what Julie had to tell them the next morning at breakfast. But when they went out and saw the hoof marks on the grass, from the window up to the pasture bars, they had to admit that Julie's ghost was only a friendly visitor who liked apples as much as she liked the girl from the city.

The Dancing Jug

A Costa Rican Ghost Story

BY LUPE DE OSMA

Once upon a time, there lived in a village up in
the mountains a man possessed by a terrible sin.
He loved money better than anything else in the
world. He had more pesos than he could count; but
the more he had, the more he wanted, and he spent
his days grasping and pinching every penny he
could.

And as soon as he had a bagful of pesos he would
exchange them for coins of pure gold. These he
would put into a big clay jug, the kind some good-
wives use to carry their water from the spring.

And his nights he spent sitting by the light of

a candle, with the golden coins piled high on a table in front of him, enraptured by their gleam and clink-clinking sound as they slipped one by one through his fingers. Ah, what a feast! What music! he thought. But because of his passion he was yellow and pinched, like a dried-up stick of wood ready for the stove.

At long last there came a day when the jug was so full of coins that it could hold no more. How his face shone with pleasure! And how he laughed, skipped, and danced for joy!

But now a problem arose for him. Where should he hide his gold? Because now he could not rest by day or sleep by night, for fear someone might steal his treasure. He thought and thought and thought — for a long time. And then one evening when the moon was not too bright, he went out into a field be-hind his house, looking around at every step to see that no one was watching. There, under a mango tree which stood by itself, he dug a hole and buried his jug, brimful of gold, marking the secret spot with a flat rock. Now, with his mind at ease, he went home, rubbing his hands and feeling very happy.

Well, this was all very fine for the yellow and

pinched miser as long as he had his health; but one day he took a chill. His condition grew steadily worse, and in three more days his thrifty life came to an end.

And what of the gold? It remained buried under the mango tree, for he had told no one of it.

But now something new came up. Shortly after the miser's funeral, there appeared one evening a curious light. A neighbor who was returning home late (it must have been midnight or thereabouts) chanced to take the path across the field where the mango tree was. Suddenly he let out a shriek and ran in terror, barefoot though he was, over brambles and pebbles. When he got home, he tumbled through the door, almost in a swoon and deathly pale. Everyone in the house jumped out of bed, asking what was the matter; and when he found his tongue, he told them how he had seen a strange greenish-blue ball of light drifting around the mango tree, and how he had stopped to look at it and heard a frightful cry.

In these small places news travels fast, and in no time the word went around that the dead miser walked as a ghost. Needless to say, from that day forward no one would go near the path after darkness fell.

Days and months passed, and when seven years had gone by the story of the light was forgotten. And now in that vicinity, a little way from the miser's house, there lived a poor lad, who was called Tomas. He was as different from the penny-pinching miser as day is from night. This poor lad earned his living by doing errands around about the village. It was very little he earned, however, and he barely managed to keep himself alive.

Now one evening when Tomas was walking home, he took the path which led through the field behind

the miser's house. It was close upon midnight and
there was no moon, but the night was clear and the
stars were bright and looked very near. By this light
Tomas could see enough to follow his way and even
trace faintly the outlines of some nearby roofs.

But since it was so late, all the houses were dark.
There was no flickering of candles, no thin light of
kerosene lamps to be seen through the open windows anywhere. Everyone in the village was in bed
and asleep. Only from far off up in the hills, where
some merry folk were celebrating, there came trail-
ing down through the air the music of a marimba,
and it mingled with the lonely call of a night bird.

Presently, and without the slightest warning,
there appeared along the path ahead of Tomas a
greenish-blue ball of light. It came slowly, steadily
. . . drifting.

"Dear me," gasped Tomas, "that's no right light!"
He stood in awe, wondering what would happen
next. The light continued to drift, till it was almost
in front of him.

In a panic, Tomas struggled to set one foot before
the other. But it was no use; his feet stood still, as
if nailed to the ground. And to make matters still

more distressing, when he tried to cry out for help his lips would not open and his tongue cleaved to the roof of his mouth.

Well, there he stood in a panic, with his arms hanging at his sides — helpless, waiting for some dreadful apparition to pounce and knock the very life out of him. And as he stood thus, wishing he were home and safe, suddenly he heard a pitiful sigh — like the sigh of a person in pain.

That was the end, Tomas thought. He fell to his knees in terror and closed his eyes, determined to see no more. But now his voice came back to him, to his surprise; and, half swooning, he managed to beg for mercy.

"Heavens! What are you?" he gasped. "What troubles you? Oh, keep away, and don't harm a poor lad that never did you hurt!"

Upon this the ghost heaved another pitiful sigh. "I am allowed to speak," said the voice of the ghost, "only to him who speaks first to me." Then the ghost went on to tell how he would not be able to rest till he found someone willing to talk with him and dig up his pot of gold.

Tomas could not keep his eyes closed any longer,

so strong was his desire to see as well as hear everything. He opened one eye, and then the other, and looked into the darkness. He saw nothing but the ball of light; though later, when he told the story, he swore he saw a white shadow floating above the greenish ball.

Finding that the light had no harm in it, he lost his terror and even ventured to offer his help, so that the poor soul might hasten to its rest.

"Then come with me, and I'll show you a big jug full of gold," said the ghost.

Well, Tomas found his courage again. He arose from his knees, felt for his machete (it was always by his side), and followed the ghost with steps so light that his feet hardly touched the ground. You would have thought they drifted like the ghost itself.

When they reached the mango tree, the ghost stopped and said, "Dig under this rock here and the jug full of gold is yours."

Tomas fell to digging furiously with his knife, and three feet down he found the jug.

"That was a true service," said the ghost. "Adios, good-by. . . . Now I can go to my rest."

"Adios!" answered Tomas. "God speed you, poor soul!" But he was too busy admiring his jug to notice the ghostly light drifting up into the darkness. Away it went and no one has ever seen it again to this day.

Tomas mopped the sweat from his brow and set to work to bring the jug out. But now something unexpected happened. Just as he stretched his arms to lift it out, the clay jug gave three hops and bounded out of the hole, all by itself. And as nimbly as you please, it bobbed up and down and from side to side, right before his eyes. Poor Tomas stood wonder-struck, his mouth agape. And the jug kept on dancing around him, as if amused by his bewilderment.

"Gracious! A jug that dances! That isn't at all as it should be!" he gasped. "This is an ugly business, I can see," he added. For he suddenly remembered that there was talk around the village of pixies having been seen in that field. "Aha! I think the pixies are in it, and I shall soon know for certain!"

And that was exactly what ailed the jug. It was bewitched! But Tomas knew a good remedy for pixies; he had learned it from his grandmother.

Quickly he took his jacket off and turned it wrong side out. The dancing jug began to hop away as if it understood what Tomas was about.

"Not so fast, my pretty!" shouted Tomas. He was not going to let his gold run away from him like that! In a twinkling he made the sign of the cross and just as quickly, he slung the jacket over the jug. No sooner was this done than the jug stopped dancing and stood as still as a clay jug should; the power of the pixies was broken. And without one bit of dread, Tomas picked it up and carried it off toward home at top speed.

When he arrived he set the jug upon a table and stretched himself out on his woven straw mat, marveling at all the strange things he had heard and seen, and wondering if perchance he were dreaming. And while turning over the thoughts in his mind, he fell asleep.

Next morning a ray of sunshine lighted up his tiny room. Tomas awoke with a jump and dashed to the table. Yes, there stood the clay jug — brimful with gold, have no doubt — as true and real as the jasmine vine winding around his window.

The Strange Visitor

BY JOSEPH JACOBS

A woman was sitting at her reel one night;
    And still she sat, and still she reeled, and
        still she wished for company.

In came a pair of broad broad soles, and sat down
        at the fireside;
    And still she sat, and still she reeled, and
        still she wished for company.

In came a pair of small small legs, and sat down
        on the broad broad soles;
    And still she sat, and still she reeled, and
        still she wished for company.

In came a pair of thick thick knees, and sat down
   on the small small legs;
  And still she sat, and still she reeled, and
   still she wished for company.

In came a pair of thin thin thighs, and sat down
   on the thick thick knees;
  And still she sat, and still she reeled, and
   still she wished for company.

In came a pair of huge huge hips, and sat down
   on the thin thin thighs;
  And still she sat, and still she reeled, and
   still she wished for company.

In came a wee wee waist, and sat down on the
   huge huge hips;
  And still she sat, and still she reeled, and
   still she wished for company.

In came a pair of broad broad shoulders, and sat
   down on the wee wee waist;
  And still she sat, and still she reeled, and
   still she wished for company.

In came a pair of small small arms, and sat down
on the broad broad shoulders;
And still she sat, and still she reeled, and
still she wished for company.

In came a pair of huge huge hands, and sat down
    on the small small arms;
    And still she sat, and still she reeled, and
    still she wished for company.

In came a small small neck, and sat down on the
    broad broad shoulders;
    And still she sat, and still she reeled, and
    still she wished for company.

In came a huge huge head, and sat down on the
    small small neck.

"How did you get such broad broad feet?" quoth
    the woman.
"Much tramping, much tramping" (*gruffly*).

"How did you get such small small legs?"
"Up late and little food" (*whiningly*).

"How did you get such thick thick knees?"
"Much praying, much praying" (*piously*).

"How did you get such thin thin thighs?"
"Up late and little food" (*whiningly*).

"How did you get such big big hips?"
"Much sitting, much sitting" (*gruffly*).

The Strange Visitor

"How did you get such a wee wee waist?"
"Up late and little food" (*whiningly*).

"How did you get such broad broad shoulders?"
"With carrying a broom, with carrying a broom" (*gruffly*).

"How did you get such small arms?"
"Up late and little food" (*whiningly*).

"How did you get such huge huge hands?"
"Threshing with an iron flail, threshing with an iron flail" (*gruffly*).

"How did you get such a small small neck?"
"Up late and little food" (*pitifully*).

"How did you get such a huge huge head?"
"Much knowledge, much knowledge" (*keenly*).

"What did you come for?"
"FOR YOU!" (*at the top of his voice, with a wave of the arm, and a stamp of the feet*).

A Shiver of Ghosts

Three Chinese Ghost Stories

BY CYRIL BIRCH

Ghosts have been encountered in all kinds of ways, some of them the most matter-of-fact imaginable. There was Sung Ting-po, for instance, who met a ghost in the early hours of the morning when he was walking to market. When he asked it who it was, it replied, "I'm a ghost."

Sung Ting-po was a stalwart young man and not given to panicking, and so when the ghost in turn asked who he was he replied, "I'm a ghost, too."

"Where are you going?" asked the ghost.

"To market," answered Sung.

"So am I," said the ghost, and they walked on together for a mile or so. Then the ghost began to complain that their progress was too slow, and suggested that they take turns carrying each other in piggy-back style. It was agreed that Sung Ting-po should have the first ride. But when it had carried him a few paces the ghost said, "How heavy you are! You're much too heavy to be a ghost."

"Well, you see," Sung explained, "I haven't been a ghost very long, and my body hasn't had time to lighten yet."

This seemed to satisfy the ghost. Soon came its turn to ride, and Sung found there was no weight to the ghost at all.

So they continued, carrying and being carried in turn. Eventually Sung Ting-po remarked, "Being a very new ghost, I don't know much about it yet. What is it that we ghosts are most afraid of?"

"There's only one thing a ghost has to fear," came the reply, "and that is to have a living man spit at one."

They came to a stream, which they decided to wade across separately. The ghost crossed first, making no sound in the water. But when Sung Ting-po tried, he made a tremendous splashing which revived the ghost's suspicions. "Why do you make such a noise?" he asked sharply.

"It's as I say, I really have very little idea of how to move about as yet," said Sung. "We new ghosts have so much to learn."

Dawn was breaking as they entered the market-place. The ghost was on Sung Ting-po's back at this point, but as it tried to get down Sung gripped it tight. It squealed and yelled but he wouldn't let it go. Grasping it firmly by the arms he brought it to the ground. But the ghost had seen the various animals waiting in the market place to be sold. As it touched the ground it changed into a sheep, no doubt with the idea of running away and losing itself in the pens nearby. Remembering what he had learned, Sung Ting-po spat at the sheep so that it would not be able to resume its ghost shape. Then he led it firmly by the neck up to a butcher, who gave him fifteen hundred cash for the sheep without a second's hesitation. This is probably the only case on record of the sale of a ghost for fifteen hundred cash.

Another ghost-catcher, Lo Ta-lin, went about his task in rather a different way. Lo was a peddler, not at all quick-witted like Sung Ting-po, but tall and swarthy and immensely strong. He had shoulders as strong as a horse. In fact, once when a friend's horse went lame he lifted it up in his own two arms and carried it back to its stable.

He was a rough fellow, and none too modest. He used to boast that he feared neither man nor devil. Only one thing he regretted, and that was that he was a poor man. He would dearly have loved to take a wife, but he had no money to buy presents and pay for the wedding. One day he was complaining to his friends in his usual surly way that a peddler's job was no better than a punishment and that he would do down to the grave without a string of cash to his name. They began to grow impatient with him, and at last one of them burst out, "You're always grumbling how little you earn, and always boasting how brave and fearless you are. You say you fear neither man nor devil. Well, then, would you be afraid of a ghost?"

Lo Ta-lin roared with laughter. "I'd like to see a ghost with a back as broad as mine," he sneered.

"Then there's one way you could earn yourself a fortune," said his friend.

"And who's going to give me this fortune?" asked Lo.

"Old Moneybags Wang, if you'll rid the Willow Lodge of whatever it is that haunts it," his friend replied.

The others gasped at the boldness of this suggestion. It was true. Old Wang would give a lot of money to be able to live in the Willow Lodge again. It was a fine mansion set in a grove of gracious willows. Wang had bought it cheap after it had stood derelict for years. He had renovated it and moved in with his family. But the next morning two of his servants were dead, mysteriously, unaccountably dead. Wang moved straight back to his old house and advertised that the Willow Lodge was to let. Three tenants in turn had taken the mansion, and each was found dead the morning after he had moved in.

Lo Ta-lin knew all this. But his eyes glinted at the thought of the reward old Moneybags might give to whomever would rid him of this ghost. He went straight round to Wang's house to put the proposition to him. Wang's servants tried to turn away this coarse fellow who came bursting in on their master, but when Lo Ta-lin flexed his huge muscles they ceased to try very hard.

Wang received Lo's offer with delight.

"There'll be a hundred strings of cash for you if you rid the Willow Lodge of this ghost," he promised. Lo's eyes gleamed brighter than ever. "And I've a nice little house by the market place," Wang added. "I'll give you that for your bride."

Lo was overjoyed. Then slowly a suspicion began to form in his mind. "How do I know that you'll keep your word?" he asked.

Wang laughed. "Very well then, we'll make a contract." And he ordered his servants to bring paper, brush and ink, and made out an agreement as follows: "In return for the service of clearing the Willow Lodge of whatever ghost, spirit or demon is at present haunting the said mansion, I, Wang Hsin-hung, do hereby undertake to give to Lo Ta-lin one hundred strings of cash together with one house in Mule Alley off the market place."

Wang signed the document and passed it to Lo Ta-lin. Lo could no more read it than fly, but he stared at it, waggling his head from side to side in pretense, then stubbed his great thumb on the ink-slab and made his mark right in the center of the paper.

That very evening Lo made his preparations.

These were very simple. They consisted of buying a number of large candles, a pound of garlic and a few pints of wine. He ground the garlic, mixed it into the wine and drank till he was just a little fuddled. Then he lit one of the candles, drew back the bolts on the outer gate of the Willow Lodge, and entered.

A large crowd had accompanied him as far as the grove of willows. A sigh went up as they saw him enter the gate. Then one man said, "I know Lo Ta-lin's plan all right. He'll wait till we've all gone, then he'll come sneaking out of that gate again. He'll hide in the grove here all night, and then sneak back in when morning comes. Then when we come and find him there he'll cook up some tale of chasing off a whole army of ghosts at midnight."

"In that case," said another, "perhaps we should make sure he doesn't get out till morning." And he bolted the gate again from the outside.

Lo Ta-lin heard the bolts crash behind him, and grunted. The light of his candle (for there was no light from the sky) made a circle round him in the courtyard. The inner gate was overgrown with creepers and brambles which Lo had to tear away.

Inside the mansion, dust lay thick in every room. It flew up as he moved, choking him, and spiders' webs clung to his face at every stop. It was a place of horror. But at last Lo Ta-lin, nothing daunted, came to a room where there was no dust, no spiders' webs. And yet the room did not look lived in; only there was a bed against one wall, complete with bed curtains and sheets no doubt left by the last tenant. Lo Ta-lin sat on the bed, snuffed out his candle and waited. He did not lie down. He did not close his eyes. He sat very still, and waited.

In the darkest and stillest hour of the night the ghost came. There was a mighty crashing outside the room. The door was flung open and the ghost rushed in. It ran round and round inside the room. Lo could only barely make it out in the gloom, for it seemed to be dressed in dark clothes and its face and hands were no lighter than its garments. Straining his eyes Lo waited until the ghost was near his bed. Then he sprang out, full in its path, and seized both its arms in his viselike grip. The ghost struggled to free itself but to no avail. Its arms were pinned to its sides and it could do nothing.

Man and ghost stood face to face. Then the ghost began to blow in Lo Ta-lin's face. Its breath was ice-

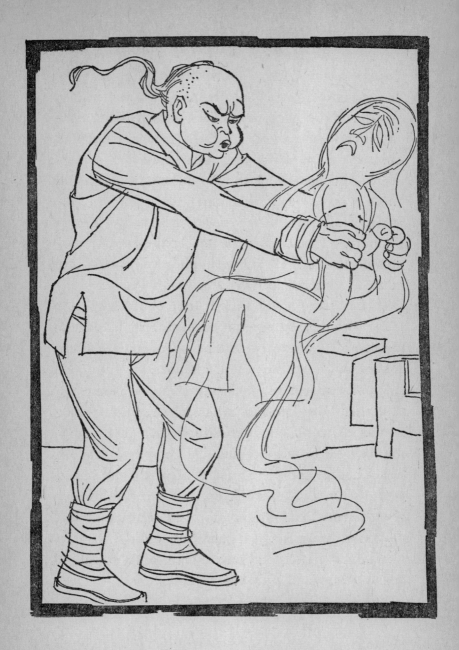

cold, fearfully cold. Lo turned his head away. But the ghost's breath continued to blow on his neck, which soon began to ache intolerably. It was just as though a knife were being driven into it. Finally Lo could bear it no longer. With a great effort he twisted his head back to face the ghost, and began to blow in his turn.

Now Lo's own breath was flavored with a good pound of garlic, and a ghost is no more capable than anyone else of standing unmoved while a pound of garlic is breathed into its face. The ghost turned its head away, and every time it tried to straighten up it met the nauseating stink of garlic. Lo kept it up until he ran out of breath. The ghost now seized its chance and blew again into Lo's face. So the strange, still battle raged between them, first one and then the other blowing on his adversary.

The long night drew painfully to its end. From somewhere in the world outside the first cock crowed. This was the moment Lo Ta-lin had been waiting for. As the cock crowed he grasped the ghost's arms even tighter than before, anxious lest it should disappear. But the ghost did not vanish. Instead, it began to shrink. There in Lo's arms it shrank and shrank. To his surprise, Lo felt the ghost's body growing harder and harder in his grasp.

At the crack of dawn Lo Ta-lin's friends had gathered in the willow grove. Now, in the morning light, they drew back the bolts and entered the mansion. Through the rank gardens and the dust-choked rooms they advanced, filled with the dread of what they might find. Their relief knew no bounds when they saw Lo at last, standing unharmed in the middle of the room. In his arms he was clutching a plank of wood. As they entered he let it go, and it clattered to the floor. They examined it curiously. It was a plank of wood from an old coffin.

"There is your ghost," said Lo, "burn it and have done."

They took the plank out and burned it. It gave off so foul a smell as it burned that no one could go near it. Old Moneybags Wang lost no time in honoring his promise to Lo of a hundred strings of cash and a house, and Lo Ta-lin lost no time in finding himself a wife and settling down with her in Mule Alley. But every time the wind blew, for the rest of his life, he suffered pains from his stiff neck, which he was never able to cure.

The important thing is not to be afraid of the ghosts one meets. An instance is the case of a man named Ts'ao who once visited a friend in Yangchow. It was the height of summer, and Ts'ao was greatly taken with his friends's cool and airy library.

"What a pleasant place this is," he remarked. "I wonder if I might be permitted to have my bed made here by the window?"

"You are most welcome to use my modest library during the day," said his host, "but I am afraid I can not allow this room to be used for sleeping." He was reluctant to give any reason for this, but Ts'ao at last obliged him to explain: "My library, I am sorry to say, is haunted."

"Haunted!" exclaimed Ts'ao. "By what?"

"By the ghost of a maidservant who hanged herself from that beam many years ago." And his host pointed upward.

But Ts'ao's desire to sleep in the library was only enhanced by this fascinating news. His host yielded, and a bed was made by the window. That night

76

Ts'ao read until late. Hardly had he put down his book and turned in than the ghost duly appeared. Ts'ao was lying with his eyes directed toward the door. Through the slit between the door and the jamb a shape appeared, no thicker than a sheet of paper. Before Ts'ao's delighted eyes it spread out into the form of a girl. She moved to the center of the room and stuck out her tongue at him. But it was no ordinary gesture of rudeness. Her head jerked, her mouth opened, and the tongue came rolling down in the manner of one who has been hanged.

"That is an interesting trick," said Ts'ao. "Please do it again."

Seeing that she had failed to scare him, the ghost paused for a moment. Then she took off her head and put it on the library table.

"Since I am not afraid of you with your head on," said Ts'ao calmly, "Why should I fear you with it off?"

The ghost had obviously exhausted her bag of tricks and disappeared.

The next morning Ts'ao told his host all that had happened. His host smiled a little uneasily and begged him to remove his bed from the library. But Ts'ao pleaded all the more urgently to remain there.

That night, at midnight, the ghost appeared again as before. But as soon as she had taken shape in the middle of the room she saw that it was the same man lying there. The ghost spat on the floor and said in disgust, "Oh, it's that stubborn fellow again," and promptly disappeared.

The Ghostly Fishermen

A French Canadian Ghost Story

BY NATALIE SAVAGE CARLSON

One summer evening in another time, some of the men of the parish were sitting in André Drouillard's yard. They had spent the day helping him to harvest his crop of hay and pile it into a big stack near his barn. So they were resting now and enjoying themselves by telling stories of fearsome and wondrous adventures they had experienced.

Albe Roberge told about the time that he had worked in a lumber camp on the Saint Lawrence River.

"It was one morning that I went off fishing by myself," he said. "I was sitting on that bank waiting

for a trout to bite when such a thing grabbed my
hook that I thought I had caught a whale. I pulled
and pulled and pulled, but it did no good. The thing
on my line was pulling just as hard as I.

"It was like a tug of war. I was being dragged
closer and closer to the water. So I braced myself
against a rock and gave one long, terrible yank. Out
flopped the biggest eel I have ever seen.

"The battle had just begun. I had to wrestle with
that eel, and what a feat of strength it was. There
was that giant eel, slippery as lard and strong as an
ox. At last I got the best of him and — "

One of his listeners interrupted.

"How did you do that," asked André Drouillard,
"if he was slippery as lard and strong as an ox?"

Albe Roberge was annoyed at this interruption.
It is not polite to break into a man's story at the
most exciting part.

"I talked to him," said Albe. "That was the
weapon I had over him. I could talk and he couldn't."

"What did you say to him?" persisted André.

Albe glared.

"I said to him, 'Little brother, why do you strug-
gle with me? I want to put you in a pot where you

80

will be warm and cozy. You will never have to go on another long trip to the sea.'

"And that is just what I did, my friends. I put him in a pot on the cookstove, and by my faith, it took five men to hold the lid on when that eel found out why he wouldn't have to go on any more long trips."

André Drouillard had yet another question.

"Just how big was that eel?" he asked.

"Fifteen — feet — long," stated Albe.

André blew out a puff of smoke from his pipe.

"Poush!" he exclaimed. "There is no such thing as a fifteen-foot eel."

Everyone gasped and there was a long silence. It is not polite to question a man's story. It makes the feeling that you think he is a liar.

"Now right here in the parish I had quite an adventure last week," boasted André.

All eyes turned to the newest storyteller. Albe Roberge and his fifteen-foot eel were forgotten.

"Yes, indeed," said André, "with my own eyes I saw the Ghostly Fishermen. And with my own ears I heard one of them crying his orders from the bow."

Everyone leaned forward to hear more because everyone knew about the Ghostly Fishermen. There could be no question of the truth here. They were three men who had gone fishing one Sunday morning instead of to church. As punishment, they and their boat had been changed into ghostly forms doomed to sail through the heavens for all eternity.

"I heard him just as plain as you can hear me," continued André. " 'To the oars! To the oars!' Those were his words. And the boat sailed so low over my head that I could have touched it — if it had been a real boat."

Albe Roberge looked at André Drouillard sullenly.

"I don't believe you saw the Ghostly Fishermen," he said rudely. "It was probably a low-hanging cloud, and the voice you heard was the cry of some water bird."

It was André's turn to be insulted. His face grew purple and he spluttered.

"You — you don't believe me. Well I — well you — you just go fishing in the river next Sunday and see what you see."

Albe sniffed.

"I will do just that thing," he promised. "What is more, I won't go to church, either. Perhaps the Ghostly Fishermen will give me a ride."

Everyone was horrified. They all begged him to give up such a daring, evil plan.

"Let him go," said André. "Let him learn that there is one straight tongue in this group."

So despite the protests and entreaties of the others, Albe Roberge set off for the river the next Sunday morning. He carried his fishing pole over his shoulder in a most determined way.

He really hoped that by some strange chance he might accidentally catch a fifteen-foot eel on his hook. Of course, he had never really seen a fifteen-foot eel — he had only wanted to make his story more interesting — but that did not mean that fifteen-foot eels did not exist.

He found a grassy place on the river bank, baited his hook, then waited for something out of the ordinary to happen. But only the most ordinary things happened to him for a while. The fish didn't bite and his worms kept falling off the hook.

Albe was disgusted. If he couldn't even catch a minnow, he wouldn't be likely to catch a fifteen-foot eel.

He had completely forgotten about the Ghostly Fishermen. He didn't give them a thought until a high, eerie cry floated up from the bend in the river.

"A bird," grunted Albe. "It is as I thought. André Drouillard is a liar."

A white filmy object slowly came around the bend. It was high in the air, above the tallest trees.

"Just as I thought," said Albe. "A cloud. That is what André Drouillard saw."

The cloud floated toward him. The cry that came to his ears was clearer.

"To the oars!" it quavered. "To the oars!"

Albe stuck his finger in his ear and wiggled it.

"That bird sounded just like somebody saying 'To the oars!' " he puzzled. "Little wonder André was fooled."

Nearer and nearer came the thing Albe called a cloud. Then the fisherman's eyes bulged like a frog's, and he dropped his pole into the water. He tried to run but his legs would not move.

That approaching image was clearly that of a boat. As it came closer, he could plainly see the three ghostly figures in it.

"To the oars! To the oars!"

The boat was right over him now. It did not slow down one bit. But a great boat hook was lowered

over the side by one of the ghosts.

It snagged into Albe's blouse and lifted him and his scared legs right up into the air. Up, up over the treetops and over the side of the boat went Albe Roberge.

Without a word, one of the figures pushed him into a seat and handed him an extra oar.

"To the oars! To the oars!" cried the coxswain of the ghostly crew.

If Albe had been frightened on the bank, he was almost mad with fear now. For as he looked down to his oar handle, his glance went right down through the bottom of the transparent boat to the bushy tops of the tallest trees.

Like one bewitched, he slowly moved the oar back and forth. Considering that it was transparent, too, it seemed unusually heavy.

The three ghostly figures paid no more attention to him. They stared into space, doubtless into eternity.

For a while Albe didn't dare open his mouth for fear that his heart would jump out of it. When he was sure that it had settled down to pounding on his ribs, he began to think. When he was able to do this clearly, he tried to plan some means of escape. If only the boat weren't so high in the sky, he might be able to jump overboard.

"Aren't we too high up to catch any fish?" he asked the ghost nearest him. "If we went lower, we might drop some lines into the river."

The man laughed with a hollow, mocking sound.

"We aren't fishing for fish," he answered. "We are fishing for lost souls."

Albe almost swallowed his tongue. He turned this idea over in his mind for a while.

"If that's what you're fishing for," he finally said, "I know just the one for you. If there is one lost soul, it is André Drouillard. If you will steer to starboard and leave the river, you will sail directly over his farm. And he must be in the yard right now because he never goes to church."

"To the oars! To the oars! To starboard! To starboard!" echoed the hollow voice of the coxswain.

The ghostly boat with the three Ghostly Fishermen and the fourth man, whose face was white enough to be that of a ghost, turned from the river and set off on a new course.

Looking through the bottom of the boat, Albe

could see the spire of the church pass underneath them. Then the winding dirt road unraveled below. There was Tante Odette's house with its two dormer windows and her outdoor oven. My faith, Jean Labadie needed some new shingles on his roof.

At last André Drouillard's neat farm drifted toward them. And most wonderful of all, there was André's big fluffy haystack.

"A little lower," Albe ordered the fishermen. "A little lower if we are to hook this lost soul down in the yard."

The boat made a long glide toward the yard of André Drouillard. The hay pile was almost directly underneath.

Albe dropped his oar, leaped over the side of the boat and went catapulting through the air. Over and over, around and around he spun, like a hawk shot on the wing.

Flop, flop he went right into the top of the haystack. He bounced up and down five times, then he dug down into the hay like a frightened badger. He could hear the voice of the Ghostly Fisherman fading into the west.

"To the oars!" lingered the mournful cry. "To the oars!"

"Ouf!" exclaimed Albe. "Put somebody else at my oar."

He stood up and brushed the hay out of his hair. He dragged himself toward the edge of the stack.

It was at this point that André Drouillard came running up with his pitchfork.

"Albe Roberge!" he shouted. "What do you mean stamping around on my horses' food? How would you like it if my horses jumped up on your table and tramped around in your soup and salad?"

Albe slid off the haystack.

"André," he cried, "an unbelievable thing has happened to me. I have just had a ride with the Ghostly Fishermen. The only way I could escape was by jumping down on your haystack."

"Yes, it *is* an unbelievable thing," scoffed André. "All of your stories are unbelievable."

No matter how well Albe explained, André would not believe his story. Nor would anyone else.

"He once said he caught an eel fifteen feet long," they would remember, and then they would shake their heads.

And as if this was not bad enough, they began spreading the story that Albe Roberge had made up this tale because he had been caught trying to pilfer some of André Drouillard's hay.

So I warn you, my friends, never tell a story about catching a fifteen-foot eel or people will not believe you if you go sailing with the Ghostly Fishermen.